This book is a work of fiction. Names, characters, places, and incidents are the product of the author's imagination or are used fictitiously. Any resemblance to actual events, locales, or persons, living or dead, is coincidental.

Miraculous™ is a trademark of ZAGTOON - Method.
© 2022 - Zagtoon - Method Animation - Toei Animation -
AB Droits Audiovisuels - De Agostini Editore S.P.A. All Rights Reserved.

Bubble images copyright © Litvinova Elena Sergeevna/Shutterstock.com

Cover design by Sammy Yuen

Hachette Book Group supports the right to free expression and the value of copyright. The purpose of copyright is to encourage writers and artists to produce the creative works that enrich our culture.

The scanning, uploading, and distribution of this book without permission is a theft of the author's intellectual property. If you would like permission to use material from the book (other than for review purposes), please contact permissions@hbgusa.com. Thank you for your support of the author's rights.

Little, Brown and Company
Hachette Book Group
1290 Avenue of the Americas, New York, NY 10104
Visit us at LBYR.com

Originally published in 2019 by Five Mile in Australia
First U.S. Edition: May 2022

Little, Brown and Company is a division of Hachette Book Group, Inc. The Little, Brown name and logo are trademarks of Hachette Book Group, Inc.

The publisher is not responsible for websites (or their content) that are not owned by the publisher.

Library of Congress Control Number: 2020941372

ISBNs: 978-0-316-42948-1 (pbk.), 978-0-316-42947-4 (ebook)

Printed in China

APS

10 9 8 7 6 5 4 3 2 1

LITTLE, BROWN AND COMPANY
NEW YORK BOSTON

ROCKFORD PUBLIC LIBRARY

Chapter 1

It's early morning in Paris, and Marinette lies spread out on her bed with her mystical companion, Tikki, curled up on her tummy. Both are sound asleep. Tikki, a bright-red Kwami with a big black spot on her forehead, is the sworn guardian of Marinette's superhero alter ego, Ladybug. Tikki has enjoyed watching over Marinette ever since the little Kwami first appeared in a burst of light and explained Marinette's new role as a superhero. Tikki also loves snuggling up with Marinette at bedtime.

Marinette's phone alarm rings, breaking the peaceful morning silence, and she sits up like a shot. Tikki is thrown from her cozy spot on Marinette's tummy, and she catapults across the room.

"*Happy birthday!*" Marinette shouts to her empty bedroom.

Tikki rights herself and flies into the air as Marinette jumps out of bed and slides down the ladder of her loft to the rest of her room. She zips across the floor on her wheely chair to her desk and taps the computer keyboard. Multiple images of Adrien surrounded by hearts appear on the screen.

Marinette sighs deeply and gazes adoringly at her screensaver. "Happy birthday, Adrien," she whispers, leaning forward to kiss the screen.

Marinette has been looking forward to Adrien's birthday for so long! She has spent hours knitting Adrien a beautiful blue scarf, and she plans to give it to him at school this morning.

Marinette picks up the carefully wrapped gift, hugs it tightly to her chest, and spins in her chair. *Finally, I have the perfect excuse to have a real conversation with him!* she thinks with delight.

The excited teenager is still close to bursting as she enters the kitchen. Marinette's mother, Sabine, is having her morning cup of tea. She looks up at her daughter.

"Marinette?" she says. "Don't forget to clean your room after school today."

Marinette's happy glow instantly fades.

"Mom," she complains, "it's Friday, and I'm already doing something with Alya this afternoon!"

"Fine," Sabine replies. "I'll go ahead and clean it, but don't blame me if I come across any of your private stuff, like your emails…your diary—"

"Okay, I'll do it, I'll do it!"

The last thing I need is for Mom to start snooping through my diary and discover I'm a secret superhero on the side, Marinette thinks, leaning forward to kiss her mother on the cheek.

"Have a nice day, sweetie."

"Happy birthday…," Marinette says, turning back from the door to grin at her mom. "Uh…I mean, have a nice day!"

• • •

Across the city, the birthday boy, Adrien Agreste, stares glumly into the bathroom mirror as he brushes his teeth. *It sure doesn't feel like my birthday*, he thinks.

Adrien had hoped his dad would come into his room this morning to wish him a happy birthday, but Adrien hasn't seen him at all and it's almost time to leave for school. He wonders if his dad has forgotten his birthday altogether.

"Happy birthday, Adrien!"

Adrien's Kwami, Plagg, hovers beside him. He's black with a long tail, pointy ears, and piercing green cat eyes. In his tiny paws, he's holding a large and very stinky piece of Camembert cheese. It's wrapped in a red ribbon. The strong, cheesy stench fills Adrien's large bathroom.

"Oh, Plagg!" Adrien cries. He pinches his nostrils to block the smell. "Get that filthy piece of Camembert out of my face!"

Plagg shrugs, throws the cheese into the air, catches it in his mouth, and swallows it in one gulp.

The fancy antique dining table in the Agreste mansion is set for twelve people, but only Adrien eats breakfast there ten minutes later. *As far as birthdays go, this one truly stinks*, he thinks.

Adrien's hopes rise as the door swings open. Although Gabriel Agreste is so busy that he never eats breakfast with his son on any day, let alone his birthday, Adrien wonders if his dad might have made time for his son today after all.

Gabriel's assistant, Nathalie, walks into the room, her high heels clicking, and Adrien slumps back over his croissant. Of course it's not his dad. He was silly to think it would be.

"Your schedule, Adrien," Nathalie says. She hands him a computer tablet.

"Thanks, Nathalie," Adrien replies. "Hey, did my father get back to you about my birthday party?"

"Well, uh…he…doesn't think it would be a good idea," Nathalie says.

"Of course not," Adrien mutters.

"Happy birthday, Adrien." Nathalie turns and walks out, leaving him alone again in the huge dining room.

Adrien pushes away his half-eaten breakfast and gets up. He's not feeling very hungry this morning.

• • •

Adrien spots Nino Lahiffe as soon as he arrives at school. Nino is waiting for him on the front steps of Collège Françoise Dupont. It's easy for Adrien to spot his best friend. Nino always has large headphones around his neck and always wears a red hat and large, round black-rimmed glasses. Adrien knows Nino wants to be a famous DJ when he grows up. He works so hard on perfecting his DJ skills! Adrien also knows Nino has no idea that Adrien is secretly the superhero Cat Noir!

Today, Nino is holding a small plastic bottle of bubble liquid. As Adrien walks toward him, Nino blows bubbles at his best friend.

"Dude!" Nino calls when he spots Adrien. "Happy birthday!"

"Thanks, man," Adrien says, grinning as he swats

at a huge bubble floating by his head. At least Adrien can count on his best friend to remember his birthday.

"Hey, what did your dad say about the party?"

"He doesn't think it's a good idea."

"Dude, seriously?" Nino says. "Has your dad always been such a downer? You'd think he'd at least remember what it was like to be young and to wanna party a little!"

"No, I'm pretty sure he was a downer back then, too." Adrien shrugs. "Well, at least I tried."

It upsets Nino to see his friend looking so bummed out. "It's your b-day, dude!" he says, putting his arm around Adrien. "Ask again!"

Adrien shakes his head. Insisting won't do any good when his dad has already made a decision.

"You know what?" Nino says, not giving up that easily. "I'm gonna have a little convo with your pops."

"Don't waste your time," Adrien says sadly. "He's not going to change his mind."

Just a few feet away, behind a low wall next to the school steps, Alya Césaire is also having a hard time trying to talk her best friend into something. Marinette holds Adrien's present in her hands as she squats beside Alya.

"You can do it!" Alya tells Marinette. "You can do it!"

"I can do it! I can do it!" Marinette repeats, a determined look on her face.

She pops up to peek over the wall, and every single bit of courage seeps out of her and onto the ground the moment she catches a glimpse of Adrien's gorgeous face. She ducks back down and shakes her head.

"I can't do it! I can't do it!" Marinette curls up in a ball and holds the present over her head, trying to shield herself from Alya's glare.

"No you don't, girl!" Alya says, her eyes narrowed and her hands on her hips. "You've been stalling all morning! Now's the time!"

Alya gives Marinette a huge shove, and before she knows what's happening, Marinette is standing in front of Adrien and Nino. She quickly hides the present behind her back with a sheepish giggle. The boys blink at her in confusion.

"Um…uh…hey," Marinette says.

"Hey," Adrien replies.

Standing at the top of the stairs with her arms

crossed, Chloé Bourgeois watches this awkward exchange and frowns. *Why would Marinette think she can talk to Adrien?* she thinks. *Her parents own a bakery!*

Chloé's father is the mayor, so Chloé believes that she is the only girl in the school good enough for Adrien Agreste. She thinks they're *destined* to be together. Chloé makes it her business to know where Adrien is and who he's hanging out with at all times.

Chloé's disgusted expression changes to one of fury when she spies the gift in Marinette's hand. Chloé spins around to confront her friend Sabrina Raincomprix, who is cowering behind her.

"Wait!" Chloé snaps at Sabrina. "Am I seeing what I think I'm seeing? Don't tell me it's Adrien's birthday!"

A trembling Sabrina consults her phone and gasps. *How did I overlook this date in the Adrien Calendar?!* she thinks.

Part of Sabrina's role as Chloé's best friend is keeping track of all Adrien's important events and occasions and making sure that Chloé is up to date with everything happening in his life.

"*Aaaagh!*" Chloé cries in frustration. "Do I have to do everything myself? Seriously, what are you good for?"

Sabrina gulps as Chloé turns and stomps off down the steps toward Adrien. Poor Marinette is still having trouble trying to explain why she is standing in front of Adrien, and she can't stop babbling. "I—uh—I wanted to, um, gift you a make!" she stammers. "I mean, gift you a give I made. I mean—"

Alya watches in horror, but Chloé decides she has heard enough.

"Outta the way!" Chloé says, walking up and roughly pushing Marinette aside. Marinette flies across the sidewalk and lands on her hands and knees. Chloé instantly adopts a sweet expression and bats her eyelashes at Adrien.

"Happy birthday, Adrien!" Chloé says. She lunges at him and kisses him loudly on the cheek.

"Uh, thanks, Chlo'."

An embarrassed Adrien gently pushes her away from him.

"Did you get the gift I sent you?" Chloé asks sweetly.

"Uh…no."

"*What?!*" Chloé cries, pretending to be really furious. "Oh, those delivery guys! I bet it was too heavy, so they had to go back and get another guy to help. Those slackers! I'll make sure they get it to you by tonight!"

She plants another noisy kiss on Adrien's cheek before slinking

away. Nino grins at his friend and gives him a friendly punch on the arm.

With a fierce look on her face, Chloé strides back over to Sabrina.

"What did you get him?" Sabrina asks in a timid voice.

"I didn't!" Chloé snarls. "*You* did!" She points a perfectly manicured finger at Sabrina's face, forcing Sabrina to pull back for fear of losing an eye. "And it better be *amazing*! And it better not be late!"

Sabrina nods, a tiny whimper escaping from her mouth.

"Ugh!" Chloé exclaims in disgust and then strides away. Sabrina follows right behind, frantically tapping a reminder into her phone.

Marinette lies facedown on the sidewalk, the present still held out in front of her. She is furious at herself. *How could I have let such a perfect opportunity*

to talk to him slip away? she thinks.

"Dummy," Marinette mumbles as she crawls back to her hiding spot beside Alya.

"Get back there!" Alya orders. "Don't be a pushover! Literally!"

Marinette groans and begins to bang the present against her head.

"Come on!" Alya says. She gives Marinette an encouraging thump on the arm. "You can do it!"

Marinette breathes in deeply and stands up just in time to see the Agrestes' long white limousine pulling up outside the school.

"Gotta go," Adrien says to Nino. "Photo shoot."

Marinette watches sadly as Adrien gets into the car. She

drops her head in defeat as the car drives away. Alya comes over to stand beside her.

Marinette turns to Alya. "Why can't I just mean what I say?" she asks miserably.

"Uh…say what you mean?" Alya asks, correcting her gently.

"*Exactly!*" Marinette cries. "Come on," she says, leading Alya toward Adrien's house.

The girls leave, and Nino watches with a determined look on his face as his friend's car drives away.

"Well," Nino says aloud to himself, "looks like I've got some business to take care of with Adrien's old man!"

Chapter 2

During the school's lunch break, Marinette pulls hard on the mailbox slot on the front wall of the Agreste mansion. Close to the Eiffel Tower, Adrien's home is surrounded by high walls and gates to keep it separated from the city. It also has high-level security, which is why Marinette and Alya are finding it impossible to do something as simple as drop Adrien's present in the mailbox.

"*Huuunhhh!*" Marinette grunts, pulling at it. "This mailbox won't budge!"

"Ring the doorbell," Alya suggests.

"Are you kidding?" Marinette cries. "What if Adrien answers and—"

With an evil grin, Alya presses the buzzer beside the gate. Marinette shrieks in alarm. A robotic camera eye shoots out of the wall above Marinette's head, and she shrieks again.

"Yes?" The girls hear Nathalie's clipped voice through a speaker below the camera.

"Umm, hi," Marinette begins. "I'm in Adrien's class and I…uh…Did I already say that? Umm—" She stops abruptly and giggles nervously as she holds up the present for the camera.

"Put it in the box!"

The mailbox slot shoots open, and Marinette places the present inside.

"Thank you," she says, giving the camera a grateful smile.

The mailbox slot slams shut, and the robotic

eye instantly snaps back into the wall, leaving Marinette and Alya blinking at each other in astonishment.

"*Oooh!*" Marinette cries, jumping up and down with excitement. "I hope he likes it!"

"You signed the note, right?"

Marinette freezes mid-jump, and her eyes almost bug out of her head as she realizes she didn't sign it.

Oh no! How will Adrien know it's from me? she wonders.

Alya sighs, dropping her head in her hands. "Girl, girl, girl…"

Marinette throws her head back and wails.

• • •

Inside the mansion, Marinette's present travels down a chute and along a conveyor belt that leads straight to an office. Nathalie retrieves the gift and sits back down at her desk.

"Who was that, Nathalie?" Gabriel Agreste's voice booms through the digital intercom on Nathalie's desk. She presses a button and her boss's face appears on the screen.

"A friend of Adrien's," she explains. "She was delivering a gift for his birthday."

"Did you remember to buy him a present from me?" Gabriel asks.

Nathalie's face drains of color. "Er…you didn't ask me to," she replies nervously.

"Of course I did!" he snaps.

"Uh—yes, Mr. Agreste," Nathalie stammers. "I'll take care of it."

"Good," he says curtly before the screen goes black.

Nathalie sighs and drops her head down onto her desk. She doesn't know what to get Adrien, and even if she did, how would she have time to organize anything? Then she spies

Marinette's beautifully wrapped gift on the desk, and a smile of relief spreads across her face.

The front-gate intercom buzzes again, briefly startling Nathalie.

She smooths her hair and presses the button. Nino's face appears on the screen.

"Yes?" she asks the boy standing outside the mansion.

"Uh...hi!" Nino says as he gives the robotic camera eye a nervous wave.

A few minutes later, Nino stands beside Nathalie in the entrance hall of the mansion.

"He'll be here in a minute," Nathalie says curtly.

Nino fiddles nervously with his bubble bottle as he waits for Gabriel Agreste. Now that Nino's actually here, he is feeling slightly less confident about trying to talk Adrien's father into anything.

Anyone who owns a sweet palace like this probably isn't the kind of dude who can be talked into anything he doesn't want to do, he thinks.

Gabriel Agreste suddenly appears at the top of the stairs.

"Adrien's not home yet," he announces loudly.

"Uhh…I was coming to see you, dude—uh, sir," Nino stammers.

"Me?" Gabriel arches one eyebrow at this young, uninvited visitor.

"Yeah, that's right," Nino continues. "Look, I know you don't want Adrien to have a party, but it's his birthday, dude—uh, I mean, sir! It's all he wants!"

"No," Gabriel says abruptly, holding up a hand to stop Nino from going on. "That's final."

"That's messed up!" Nino says, not noticing that Adrien has just walked in the door behind him. "He never screws up in class. He always does whatever you tell him! Photo shoots, fencing, Chinese, piano…"

Adrien is both happy and horrified to find his best friend in his house, appealing to his dad. He walks over and places a hand on Nino's shoulder.

"Nino," he says quietly. "You're here."

Nino turns and grins at Adrien.

"Anything for my best bud," he says, then turns back to Gabriel. "Show some awesomeness, du— I mean, sir! Please?"

Gabriel stares coldly at Nino from the top of the staircase.

"Forget it, Nino," Adrien says quietly. "Really, it's fine."

"Listen, young man," Gabriel says sternly. "I decide what's best for my son. In fact, I've just decided you're a bad influence and you're not welcome in my house ever again! *Leave now!*"

"Father!" Adrien is shocked by how rude his dad is being to his friend. "He was just trying to do something cool for me!"

But Gabriel simply ignores his son and turns and walks away. Nathalie steps in front of the two boys and glares at Nino.

"Goodbye!"

Realizing he's lost, Nino's expression changes from fear to anger. He turns and storms out the front door.

"Nino, wait!" Adrien chases his friend and grabs his arm outside the door. "I'm sorry. My father, he's...pretty stubborn. It's just best to stay out of his way."

"It's not fair, Adrien!" Nino says angrily, batting Adrien's hand away. "Harsh! Uncool!"

He hurries down the front steps, leaving Adrien alone and feeling more miserable than ever.

"Thanks anyway, Nino," Adrien says quietly. *Some birthday*, he thinks as he watches his friend leave.

• • •

In the nearby park, Nino flops down on a bench and pulls out his plastic bottle of bubbles. He tries to calm himself down by blowing bubbles and watching them float out across the park.

"But, Daddy, *pleeeeeease!*"

Nino hears a child wailing nearby. He looks around and sees a young boy being pulled along through the park by his father.

"No!" the father says sternly, pulling the child away from the playground. "It's not playtime! You've got your chores to do."

Nino frowns and shakes his head as he watches them leave. "Adults ruin everything," he mutters to himself. *"All the time!"*

• • •

From within his secret lair, hidden high above Paris, the master supervillain Hawk Moth chuckles as he senses Nino's anger in the city far below.

"Desperate to help his friend but feeling powerless," he says, his deep voice echoing around the large room. "How frustrating. It won't be long before frustration turns to anger!"

Hawk Moth's ultimate goal is to steal Ladybug's and Cat Noir's Miraculouses. But to do so, he needs the energy of negative emotions. The moment he detects someone's anger, bitterness, or sadness, he seizes the opportunity to use their energy to his advantage. Nino's rage is exactly this kind of opportunity.

The tall, sleek Hawk Moth clutches his thin, black stick in gloved hands. A silver mask covers his head, leaving only his eyes and evil grin visible. He closes his eyes as thousands of white butterflies flutter around him. A panel in the wall slides back to reveal a large, round window. A glowing white butterfly flies down to land on Hawk Moth's palm.

He places his other hand over the butterfly. Black spots flood into his palm, transforming the butterfly into a dark-purple moth with bright-white accents. It is identical in shape to the outline of the moth on his mask.

"Fly away, my little akuma," Hawk Moth says, lifting his hand and setting the purple moth free. "And evilize him!"

The now-evil akuma flies out the window and down to the streets of Paris.

• • •

Nino is still blowing bubbles on the park bench and looking annoyed when the akuma approaches him.

Enchanted so that it can combine with any object, the akuma flies down, lands on the plastic bottle of bubbles in Nino's hand, and disappears into it. The brightly colored bottle turns a deep black as a mysterious force takes hold of Nino. He raises his head and grits his teeth, a fierce look in his eyes. Hawk Moth's deep voice vibrates inside Nino's mind.

"Hawk Moth is my name," the deep voice says, *"and Bubbler is now yours!"*

The beginnings of a mask appear on Nino's face as he listens.

"I will help you with these horrid adults," Hawk Moth continues. *"And all you have to do in return is help me get something from Ladybug and Cat Noir."*

"Yes, Hawk Moth," Nino answers, an evil grin spreading across his face.

A wave of black and purple covers Nino and begins to transform him. A suit of red, yellow, and blue bubbles covers Nino's body, with a target on his chest. His face is blue, and instead of his hat, a peaked red headpiece now sits on his head. Strapped to his back is an oversize bubble bottle containing a large, yellow bubble wand with two hoses that connect to the front of the suit.

Nino is now an evil villain—the Bubbler!

Chapter 3

The Bubbler shoots up into the air across Paris and lands on a rooftop, bubbles flying out behind and around him.

"No more adults means total freedom!" the Bubbler cries. "This is *so sweet*!" He grabs the oversize wand from behind him. *"Off the hook!"*

The Bubbler dives off the top of the building and flies over the city of Paris. A long line of large purple bubbles trails out behind him.

There is confusion on the streets below as Parisians watch the large purple bubbles float down onto sidewalks, into stores, and through open windows. Confusion quickly turns to horror as the bubbles begin to surround all the adults in the city. Startled grown-ups find themselves trapped inside the large bubbles, which turn green and float up into the sky. Parents in the park grab their children and run as fast as they can, but there is no escaping the enchanted bubbles. Frightened children cry and shout as they watch their beloved parents, relatives, and teachers float away from them.

Before long, the skies of Paris are filled with large green bubbles containing worried-looking adults.

Hawk Moth watches the bubbles float past his window and smiles at the Bubbler's work.

"Perfect," Hawk Moth says with an evil grin.

• • •

Home for lunch, Marinette pushes the peas on

her plate around with her fork and into the shape of a heart.

"Adrien must have gotten his gift by now," she murmurs, a dreamy smile on her face.

"What's that?" Sabine asks.

Marinette freezes. She was so distracted thinking about Adrien that she hadn't noticed her mom come in behind her.

Marinette spins around on her stool. "Uh… just that I can't wait to get back to school this afternoon!"

Sabine chuckles as she opens the terrace doors to let some of the lovely spring air into their apartment. She doesn't notice the large purple bubble floating toward her until it's too late. Marinette gasps in horror as the bubble enters through the open window and engulfs her startled mother. The bubble turns green and carries Sabine through the door and up into the sky.

"Mom!" Marinette cries, running out onto the terrace. *"Mooooom!"*

From the terrace, Marinette can see dozens of similar green bubbles floating up, all carrying adults—including her father!

"Dad!"

"Your parents!" Tikki hovers behind her. "Hawk Moth must have released another akuma!"

"I've got to find his newest villain ASAP!" Marinette says, watching her poor parents float up into the sky.

Marinette runs back into the apartment and out of sight, knowing it's up to her to stop this.

"Tikki! *Spots on!*"

Tikki turns into an energy stream and flows into Marinette's earrings. The earrings turn red and grow five black spots as Marinette's transformation into Ladybug begins. In a cloud of stars and sparks, her body is covered in a red suit with black polka dots. A red-and-black mask appears, covering Marinette's eyes and protecting her true identity.

Now, transformed into the miraculous Ladybug, she's ready to take on this latest villain!

• • •

On the streets of Paris, hundreds of large green bubbles rise and float above the Eiffel Tower. The Bubbler stands back and admires his work from a rooftop.

"And now," he says with a grin, *"party time!"*

Ladybug runs out of her apartment and looks up to see the Bubbler's face on a cluster of purple bubbles overhead. He addresses the kids and teenagers on the streets below.

"Hey, hey, hey! Today's your lucky day, little dudes." His voice echoes through the half-empty streets. "The adults have taken the day off, so make the most of it!"

Beside Ladybug, two young children and a teenager gaze up at the bubbles with scared looks on their faces.

"No chores," the Bubbler continues, "no homework, no more nagging. Just *fun, fun, fun, fun*! This is the Bubbler's gift to you!"

The little boy bursts into tears, and Ladybug leans down to comfort him and his sister. "Don't worry," she says kindly. "Your parents will come back. I'll see to it!"

She stands up and faces the teenager. "You take care of them in the meantime."

"*Yay!*" they cry as they watch Ladybug sprint away and leap up onto the roof of a nearby building. *"Go Ladybug!"*

• • •

Back at Adrien's mansion, the birthday boy is eating his lunch all alone in the dining room. He takes one last bite and wipes his mouth with a thick white napkin.

"Wow," he says sarcastically. "That was a birthday lunch break to remember. Yay!"

He fist-pumps the air limply, sighs, and grabs his bag to head back to school.

The house is deathly silent as Adrien walks into the entrance hall. No servants and no Nathalie in sight.

That's weird, he thinks. *It's the middle of the day. Where are all the adults?*

"Nathalie?" Adrien calls. "Father?"

There is no answer.

Feeling miserable, Adrien opens the front door to an unexpected sight. A crowd of kids from school, including Chloé and Sabrina, are gathered outside his house in the courtyard at the bottom of the steps. Behind them are two long tables covered with party food and drinks. A stage, a DJ mixing board, party lights, and giant speakers are set up at the far end.

"Yay!" the crowd cheers. *"Happy birthday!"*

Adrien stares down at the scene before him, completely shocked.

"Hey, hey, hey, birthday boy!"

The Bubbler floats above Adrien on a large purple bubble, a wicked grin on his blue face.

"Guess what?" he says. "Daddy's *gone*! While the cat's away, the mice will play!"

Despite his new supervillain getup, Adrien recognizes his friend's voice immediately.

"Nino!" he cries, his eyes wide with shock.

"The Bubbler's brought all your homies together for one single, sole purpose," the villain continues. "To *cel-e-brate*!"

"Yeah!" The crowd of teenagers cheers again.

The Bubbler swoops down to the DJ mixing board. "Let's get this party started!" he shouts into the microphone as he scratches the record. Loud pop music fills the courtyard outside Adrien's usually silent mansion.

Adrien watches for a moment as the crowd begins to dance. Then he turns and runs back inside the house.

"Come on, everybody!" the Bubbler shouts. "I brought you here to party! So keep dancing, or you'll join the adults up in the sky!"

Some of the teenagers look upset about being threatened, not to mention having their parents taken away from them. But no one is brave enough to say anything to the Bubbler. They don't want to end up floating above the city streets, too!

The Bubbler laughs maniacally and sets off fireworks that explode into bubbles over the Agreste mansion.

Back in his lair, Hawk Moth chuckles, thrilled with how events are unfolding down in the city.

"It won't be long before Ladybug and Cat Noir show up to meet their doom!"

Hundreds of white butterflies flutter around

Hawk Moth as the master villain spreads his arms and laughs loudly.

• • •

Adrien closes his bedroom door, ready to transform into Cat Noir, but he pauses as he stares down at his Miraculous. He can't stop thinking about the party going on downstairs and how good it felt to have people there to celebrate his birthday with him.

Plagg notices that Adrien is hesitating and takes the opportunity to make a little mischief.

"What's your problem?" Plagg taunts. "Relax! You're getting the party you've always wanted!"

Like Tikki, Adrien's Kwami is small, but Plagg is much naughtier than Marinette's Kwami.

"But Nino's been akumatized!" Adrien is torn between wanting to do the right thing and wanting to enjoy his birthday party. "I've gotta help him!"

"You may never get this chance again!" Plagg's

eyes twinkle. "Come on! Let's have a little fun while your father's away. Then we'll save Nino, trap his akuma…and all will be good!"

The hurt and loneliness Adrien has been feeling all day rise to the surface. He suddenly has a strong desire to disobey his absent father.

"Okay," Adrien says, a determined expression on his face. "You're right. This might be the first day in my life that I get to do what I want for once!"

Chapter 4

*L*adybug leaps across the Paris rooftops, only pausing when she spots bubble fireworks exploding over the Agreste mansion.

"It's you and me, Bubbler," she says, angrily clenching her fists at the thought of her poor parents trapped inside those horrible bubbles.

She launches herself off the building and continues toward the unsuspecting villain.

• • •

Meanwhile, Adrien is getting into the spirit of the party. He dances alongside his guests, shimmying and punching the air with glee. "Yeah!"

Caught up in the music and the atmosphere, Adrien doesn't notice the miserable expressions of his classmates. He sidles up to one of the girls, who stares sadly at the ground and looks as if she is dancing on autopilot.

"Hey, nice party," he shouts over the music. "I guess…since it's my first one."

The girl gives him two thumbs-up and forces a smile for the birthday boy, but her face falls again the moment she turns away. This time Adrien does notice, and as he looks around the party, he frowns when he sees similar expressions on other kids' faces.

This doesn't look right, he thinks. *Shouldn't people be happy and smiling at a party?*

He may not have been to one before, but he's pretty sure that cheery expressions are one of the main ingredients for an awesome party!

Over by the mixing board, Chloé pushes Sabrina toward the Bubbler.

"Um...," Sabrina says hesitantly. "I'm requesting a slow dance?"

"It's a bit early for that, isn't it?" the Bubbler shouts back.

"Uhh..." Sabrina blinks nervously, not sure what to say next.

"Agh!" Chloé rolls her eyes and steps forward, elbowing Sabrina out of the way.

"It's for Adrien," Chloé coos in her sweetest voice. "His first slow dance...." She purses her lips and bats her eyes at the Bubbler.

"*Ohhh!*" the Bubbler cries, grinning back at Chloé. "You know it, girl!"

He switches the track to a slow song, and people automatically turn to one another and begin to dance in pairs. Adrien watches the crowd in confusion while Chloé slinks up to stand beside him.

They look like robots! Adrien thinks. *Like they're programmed to keep dancing and partying even if they don't want to!*

"Is it me?" he asks Chloé. "Or does everyone seem a bit weird?"

"Forget about them!" Chloé says, grabbing his arm and yanking him onto the dance floor for the slow dance. "Let's go dance! Come on!"

• • •

From her position on top of the wall that surrounds Adrien's mansion, Ladybug watches the Bubbler at the mixing board as he bobs his head and grins at the teenagers dancing below.

Ladybug is about to leap down and confront him when she sees something that makes her blood run cold.

Adrien has his arms around Chloé's waist....Chloé has her arms around his neck....They are...slow dancing together!

Ladybug watches with horror as Chloé leans up to kiss Adrien on the cheek. He pulls away just in time, but it's enough to convince Ladybug to act.

"There is no way this is happening!" she says out loud, knowing there's only one thing that can help her. *"Lucky Charm!"*

Ladybug throws her yo-yo up into the sky and hundreds of ladybugs fly out. Ladybug waits for them to transform themselves into a mystery object, which she can use to stop the total disaster that is Chloé dancing with—and possibly *kissing*—Adrien!

Once Ladybug uses this power, her earrings will begin to flash and the five black spots on them will disappear one by one. After five minutes, when all the black spots have faded, she will turn back into Marinette. But Ladybug is too upset to worry about that now. She *cannot* let Chloé kiss Adrien!

A vinyl record drops into Ladybug's hands.

"A record?" She frowns. *"Hmmm."*

Ladybug can see the Bubbler rummaging through the records behind his mixing desk, and her super senses spring into action. She surveys every part of the courtyard below her: the turntable, the record control switch, and the side wall of the mansion.

Aha! She's got it!

Ladybug spins on the spot, releasing the record from her hands. It flies through the air, bounces off the side wall, hits the control switch, and lands on the turntable. There, it begins to spin, changing the slow song to a fast one. The couples step apart and start dancing separately again. Adrien peels Chloé's hands off his shoulders, steps back, and begins to dance.

The Bubbler frowns. "Dude!" he says. "Who just hijacked my mix?"

"Yours truly!" Ladybug announces proudly. Before she can continue, her earrings start beeping; it's the signal that there is only one black spot left.

"Huh?" She gasps. "Better bug out quick before I change back to normal!"

She somersaults off the high wall and lands on her feet on the street outside Adrien's home.

"Spots off!"

Tikki falls into her open palms as Ladybug

transforms back into Marinette.

"Marinette…," Tikki says weakly.

Tikki's energy is always depleted after she has transformed Marinette into a superhero. The tiny creature can barely open her eyes as she rubs her little head.

"It was an emergency!" Even as Marinette says the words, she knows it's not really true. She is suddenly wracked with guilt as she cradles her exhausted Kwami.

"Yeah," Tikki says, forcing her huge violet eyes open to look at Marinette. "If by *emergency* you mean *jealousy*! You know what happens once you use your Lucky Charm! You only have minutes before—"

"I turn back," Marinette says. "I know, but I figured…the Bubbler…he's not going anywhere!"

Tikki blinks up at Marinette. She is clearly disappointed in her friend.

"We have time to get you some food to get your energy back up," Marinette continues. "Then we'll get right back out there. I promise!"

With Tikki safely back in her purse, Marinette returns to the courtyard of the mansion. The teens are still dancing, so Marinette quickly walks over to one of the tables. She swipes some cookies and sneaks them into her bag for Tikki to munch on and get her energy back. Then she looks around for somewhere to transform back into Ladybug.

"I've gotta find a place where I can transform," Marinette mutters to herself. "Fast!"

"Where have you been, girl?"

Marinette turns to find Alya standing behind her with a worried expression.

"I was so scared something had happened to you!" Alya says, stepping forward to give her best friend a hug.

"Me too!" Marinette says, squeezing her back.

"I'm sure Ladybug and Cat Noir will show up in a minute to save us all," Alya says. "They've never failed us! In the meantime, come with me. I've got something for you!"

"Uhh…there's something I have to do first," Marinette says, gesturing in the opposite direction.

Alya smiles. "It's about Adrien…," she teases.

Alya starts to walk away and Marinette feels torn. *I have to focus on stopping the Bubbler*, she thinks. *But surely it couldn't hurt to put it off for just a tiny bit longer.*

"Okay," she says, hurrying after Alya.

Tikki pokes her head out of the purse, a half-eaten cookie in her hand. "Marinette!" she scolds. "The Bubbler!"

"Okay, okay," Marinette says. "In a sec!"

• • •

Nearby, the Bubbler walks up to a teenage boy

named Ivan. Ivan is leaning against the wall, and he looks utterly miserable.

"Hey, you!" the Bubbler demands. "Why aren't you having fun?"

"None of your business," Ivan snaps.

The Bubbler's expression darkens. "Then I'm gonna make it my business!"

Ivan gasps and steps back in fright as the Bubbler reaches for his bubble wand.

• • •

Inside the mansion, Alya leads Marinette straight to Nathalie's office. The two girls poke their heads into the large room.

"Look!" Alya whispers, pointing at the gift Marinette left, still sitting on Nathalie's desk. "Now you can sign your gift!"

"*Yes!*" Marinette says. She quickly grabs a pen off the desk and scribbles a birthday message with her name on a note. "'Love, Marinette.' There!"

She rips off the note and sticks it on the gift. She holds it up proudly and gives it a little kiss for extra luck.

Tikki, her energy back, pops out of the purse. "Right, we're good!" she says firmly. "Spots on, Marinette!"

"I can't do it now," she whispers, looking around anxiously. "Alya's here!"

"What'd you say?" Alya says, poking her head

back into the room from her lookout post outside the door.

"Um…" Marinette beams a big grin at Alya. "You go ahead! I'll meet you in the yard!"

Alya nods and disappears, closing the door behind her.

"Phew!" Marinette sighs with relief. But then she hears a bubbling noise and turns to see a large green bubble with Ivan trapped inside float past the office window.

"No!" Marinette cries. "You were right, Tikki! I never should have waited this long!"

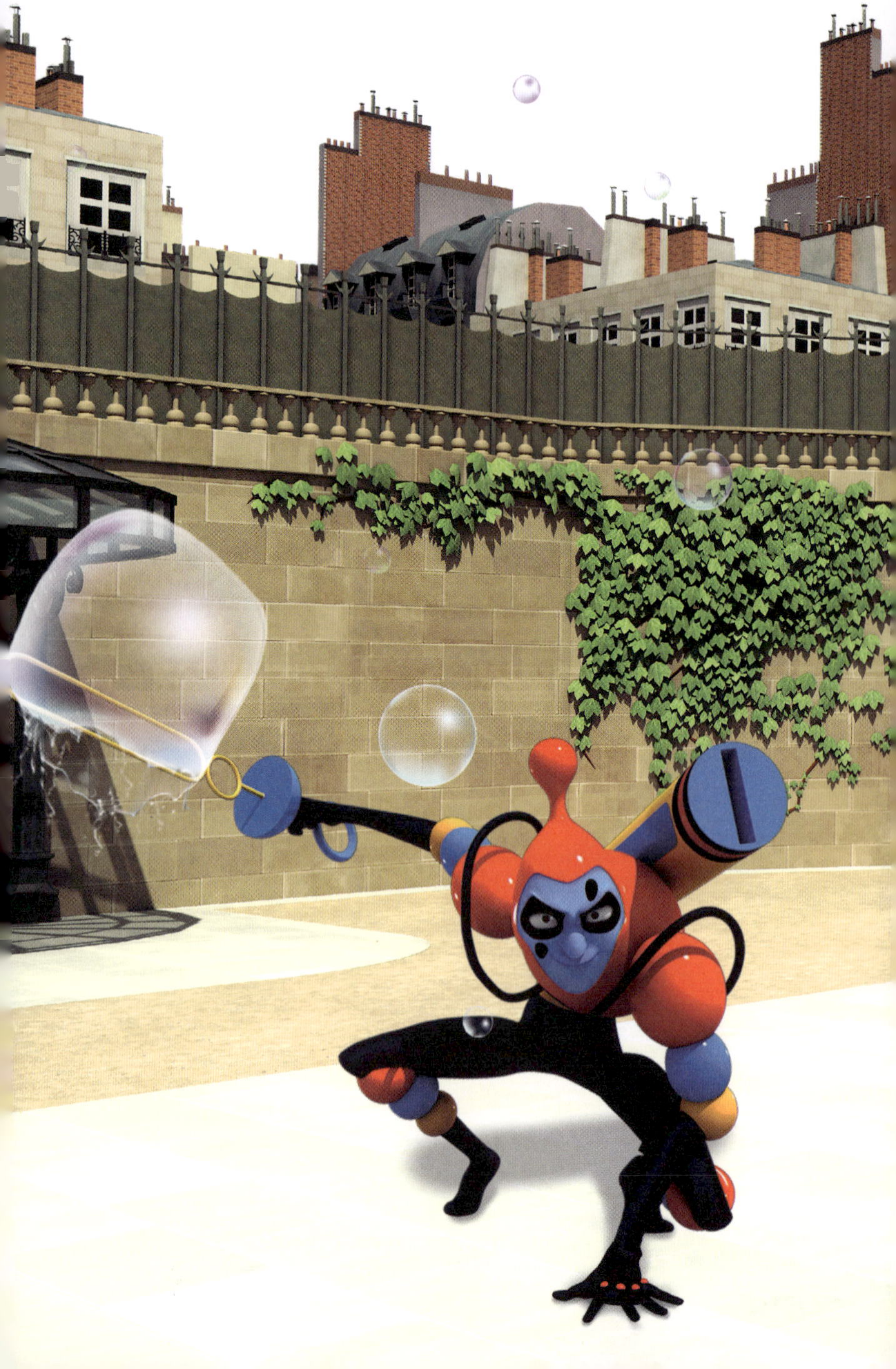

Chapter 5

Adrien is onstage, holding a microphone. The Bubbler stands behind him, watching the crowd with a stern expression.

"Hey, Paris!" Adrien shouts happily into the microphone. "How ya doin'?!"

A few of the guests manage feeble responses: "Yeah…" "Good…I guess…" But it's mostly a collection of glum faces that stares back at the birthday boy.

The Bubbler leans forward and growls at the crowd. He reaches for his bubble wand as a silent warning. The terrified guests plaster on fake smiles, raise their hands, and cheer loudly.

"Yeah! Woohoo!" they shout, trying to muster up some enthusiasm.

Adrien cheers along with the crowd, until he glances up to see Ladybug standing on the high wall, hands on her hips. The rest of the crowd follows his gaze and gasps and points up at the superhero.

"Ladybug?" Adrien says.

Ladybug flings her yo-yo at the power strip plugged into the mixing desk. It knocks the plug from the socket, instantly killing the music. Ladybug gracefully catches the yo-yo in one hand as it swings back up to her.

"Sorry, Bubbler," she says, "but the party's over!"

"Why you gotta be like that?" the villain whines.

"You made all the adults disappear—that's why!" Ladybug says sternly. "And now you're imprisoning anyone who isn't having fun!"

Adrien realizes the mistake he's made and sprints back inside the house. He has to help Ladybug stop this villain.

"You will not bust my party!" the Bubbler shouts at Ladybug, reaching behind him for his bubble wand.

Using his wand, the Bubbler fires a wave of red bubbles at the spotted superhero, but Ladybug spins her yo-yo so quickly that it acts as a shield. Ladybug deflects all the bubbles, and then she leaps upward off the wall.

The Bubbler launches himself off the ground, and the superhero and villain fly into the air to face off against each other as the people below scream and run for cover. The force of the bubbles making contact with Ladybug's shield propels them both backward and through the sky. They each land with a loud thud on opposing party tables.

Inside the house, Adrien shuts his bedroom door behind him and opens his pocket for Plagg to fly out.

"I think I've been a complete idiot," he says, feeling ashamed. "Plagg, *claws out!*"

"*Aaah!*" Plagg groans as he turns into an energy stream that flows into Adrien's Miraculous ring. A tight black suit and tail, boots, cat ears, and a mask replace Adrien's clothes, transforming him into superhero Cat Noir! He wields a black staff and is now ready to take on the Bubbler alongside Ladybug.

Back in the courtyard, Ladybug flings her yo-yo toward the Bubbler, but it bounces off a red bubble and springs back at her.

Suddenly, Cat Noir is standing beside Ladybug. Using his staff, Cat Noir knocks the yo-yo out of the way before it can strike his partner.

Cat Noir arches an eyebrow at Ladybug, a smile on his face. He looks very pleased with himself. "Looks like I made it just in time!" he boasts.

"I had it under control," Ladybug says, rolling her eyes at him.

The yo-yo plummets back toward them and

hits Cat Noir right on the head!

"But thanks!" Ladybug grins as Cat Noir rubs his sore spot.

The Bubbler's fury grows as he watches this exchange. The outline of a purple moth mask appears over his eyes, and he listens to Hawk Moth's voice inside his head.

"*Get their Miraculouses!*" he commands. *"I want those powers. Now!"*

Spurred on by Hawk Moth's command, the Bubbler grabs his bubble wand and lets out a war cry. *"Aaaaggghhhhhhh!"*

Holding the wand out in front of him, the Bubbler spins on the spot, firing hundreds of red bubbles from his weapon. The bubbles shoot quickly toward the superheroes, forcing Ladybug and Cat Noir to use their yo-yo shield and spinning staff to fight the bubbles off.

Finally, when every bubble has been deflected

and is floating away into the sky, Ladybug and Cat Noir turn triumphantly to face the Bubbler. But the smug look on his face confuses them. They quickly understand as the Bubbler snaps his fingers, and the red bubbles freeze, turn green, and descend on Ladybug and Cat Noir at a rapid rate.

The green bubbles begin to swirl around the two superheroes like a spinning tornado, eventually forming one giant bubble that traps Ladybug and Cat Noir inside.

The frightened party guests watch from their hiding spots behind the columns that surround the front of the Agreste mansion.

"Give me your Miraculouses before you run out of air!" the Bubbler orders.

"Dream on, Bubbler!" Ladybug says.

"Total party poopers!" he cries, shaking his head. "Just like *adults*!"

"Kids *need* adults!" Ladybug shouts.

"*False!*" the Bubbler cries angrily. "Kids need freedom! Fun! Let loose and live it up! Adults are controlling and bossy!"

"But adults keep children safe and protected," Ladybug insists. "They *care* for their kids! They *love* them!"

Many of the teenagers watching nod in agreement with Ladybug. However, inside the bubble, Cat Noir frowns as he listens to his partner defending the grown-ups.

"Most adults do, anyhow," he mutters to himself. Then he shouts at the Bubbler. "You *must* bring the adults back!"

"Nope, *never*!" the Bubbler shouts back. "You know what? Since you care about these adults so much, why don't you go float with them for a while?!"

The Bubbler runs at the green bubble, holding his wand out in front of him. With one swish of the wand, he launches the giant bubble high up into the sky, as easily as hitting a ball with a bat.

"*Aaahhhhh!*" the superheroes cry as they fly upward in their bubble prison.

The guests below scream as they watch their only hope of rescue disappear into the clouds.

Pleased with himself, the Bubbler smiles until Hawk Moth's angry voice echoes inside his head. "*What do you think you're doing, Bubbler!*" he scolds. "*You're supposed to seize their Miraculouses!*"

• • •

High above Paris, Ladybug and Cat Noir are helpless inside their bubble prison. They use their boots to push against the sides, but the bubble is too solid for them to burst.

Ladybug has an idea. She turns to Cat Noir. "Use your Cataclysm!"

"Couldn't you have said that five hundred feet ago?!" he asks in frustration.

"We can't stay stuck in this bubble together forever!" Ladybug replies.

Cat Noir grins and raises his eyebrows at Ladybug, thinking, *But wouldn't it be nice if we could?*

Ladybug groans. The last thing she needs is to be stuck in a bubble with the arrogant Cat Noir for eternity. Now if it were Adrien...that might be a different story.

Cat Noir springs into action.

"*Cataclysm!*" he shouts, holding out his hand and summoning his own special power. A cloud of black particles forms in his palm and charges it with magical energy. Cat Noir now has the power to destroy anything he touches, a useful skill if you need to pop a giant enchanted bubble!

Cat Noir rests his hand against the wall of the bubble and it bursts immediately. The superheroes fall through the air and toward the ground at breakneck speed.

"Should we see if you land on your feet this time?!" Ladybug shouts to Cat Noir as they continue to nose-dive through the air.

"No, thanks!" Cat Noir calls back, not sure that even a superhero with his nimble cat reflexes could land upright from this height!

Ladybug turns her head and sees that they are falling alongside the Eiffel Tower.

"Your stick!" she calls to Cat Noir, pointing at the tower. "There!"

"Got it!" Cat Noir cries.

He reaches behind him for his staff and hurls it with all his strength at the side of the tower. The stick flies through the air before attaching itself firmly to the Eiffel Tower's iron frame.

"Hang on!" Ladybug grabs Cat Noir's arm and flings her yo-yo at the stick. The string loops itself around the staff and, with Ladybug still holding tightly to it, acts as a bungee cord. The two superheroes are catapulted up into the air before swinging back down.

Ladybug pulls on the string to release the stick, and they both fall the remaining distance to the ground.

"*Aaahhhhhh!*" they cry as they somersault a few times before eventually sliding to a halt.

"Good thing cats aren't afraid of heights," Cat Noir says with a smirk.

Ladybug throws his wand back to him. "We've

got to get to his bubble wand," she says firmly. "That's gotta be where the akuma is!"

Cat Noir's ring starts to beep, and one of the claws on its glowing green cat paws blinks and disappears. "We'd better hurry!"

Like Ladybug's Lucky Charm, Cat Noir's Cataclysm begins a countdown on his ring that will transform him back into Adrien in five minutes.

The two superheroes sprint back toward Adrien's house as fast as they can.

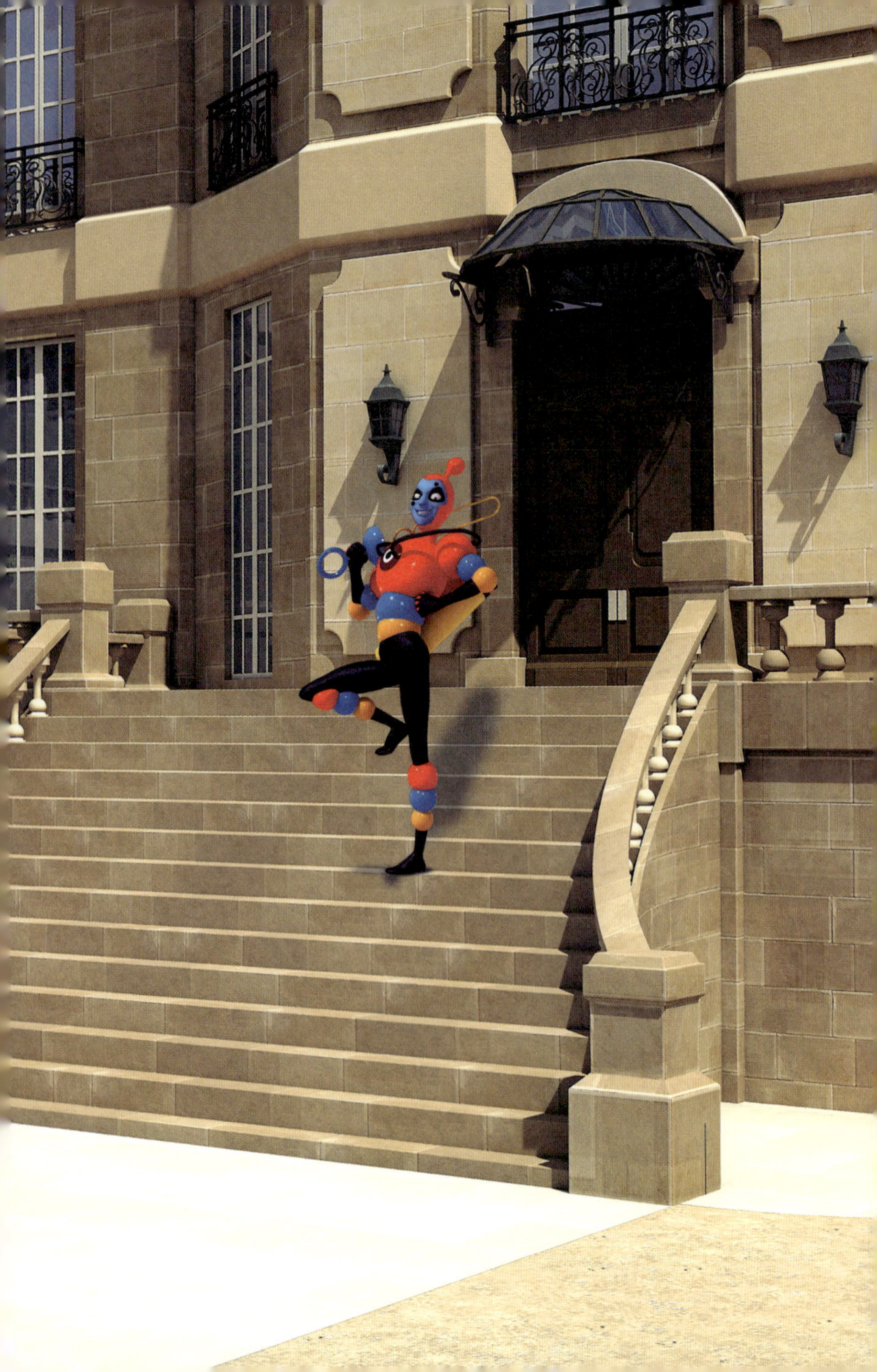

Chapter 6

The Bubbler looks out across the empty courtyard. All the terrified teenagers continue to cower behind the small columns lining Adrien's front steps.

"Where is everybody?" he cries angrily. "Get out here and party!"

"Sorry to burst your *bubble*!"

The Bubbler spins around to see Ladybug standing on the high front wall behind him, with Cat Noir beside her.

Alya, hiding with the other teens, stands up and points at the superhero. *"Ladybug!"*

The relieved teenagers all begin to chant. "Ladybug! Ladybug! Ladybug!"

Ladybug looks down at the villain and smiles. "No one wants to party with you anymore, Bubbler!"

"What's wrong with all you guys?" the villain asks the guests, confused by their attitude. "Why you gotta be such haters?!"

His confusion turns to anger, and with one swoosh of his bubble wand, the Bubbler sends a barrage of large purple bubbles at the teenagers, trapping each of them inside a bubble.

"*Nooo!*" Ladybug and Cat Noir shout as the bubbles turn green and lift off the ground toward the sky, their screaming friends and classmates trapped inside.

"Outer space is the next stop for your precious peeps," taunts the Bubbler. "And they're never coming back!"

He shoots upward and begins leaping from

rooftop to rooftop, with Ladybug and Cat Noir in close pursuit behind him.

The Bubbler leaps onto the Eiffel Tower. He clings to the wrought-iron lattice of the tower and shoots explosive red bubbles down at the two superheroes as they climb up toward him. But Ladybug and Cat Noir dodge the bubbles, making the Bubbler even angrier.

The Bubbler vaults halfway up the Eiffel Tower to a landing. Ladybug and Cat Noir follow close behind to face off against the villain. The Bubbler shoots another red bubble at them, and they jump out of the way just in time. It explodes in a fiery ball behind them.

Cat Noir's ring beeps again, and he looks down to see that there is only one paw left.

"I'm gonna switch back soon!" he shouts to Ladybug. "Hurry!"

Without a second to spare, Ladybug throws her yo-yo up into the sky. Lucky Charm is her last chance to save everyone.

"*Lucky Charm!*" the superhero cries.

Hundreds of ladybugs fly out as the yo-yo is released. Ladybug waits for them to transform into a mystery object she can use to stop the Bubbler.

A giant red-and-black wrench falls down into the superhero's hands. "Huh?" she asks, frowning.

"Your…plumbing skills are gonna help us out?" Cat Noir asks, still making lame jokes even in the face of danger.

The Bubbler unleashes a torrent of deadly bubbles at Cat Noir, who bounces and hops all over the tower, narrowly avoiding the flames that erupt as the bubbles make contact with the structure.

"Your aim could use a little work!" Cat Noir taunts from his position high above the Bubbler. "Is that all you got?"

Ladybug's super senses spring into action, and she takes in every element around her on the landing: a fan vent, a plumbing pipe, a bolt. She glances back down at the wrench. "Got it!" she says.

As Cat Noir continues to dodge the bubbles, Ladybug runs over and, with the wrench, loosens the bolt connecting the pipe to the fan vent. The pipe comes loose and begins to flap around in the air, releasing a strong gush of steam from its open end.

"Cat Noir," she calls. "Cover me!"

Cat Noir wrestles the flapping pipe down to the landing. He holds it firmly in his grasp as it continues to release steam.

"Go on!" he calls to Ladybug, pointing the pipe toward the Bubbler.

The Bubbler sends another blast of bubbles at Cat Noir, but this time the air from the pipe blows them away. Furious, the Bubbler raises his bubble wand high above his head, ready to unleash another wave of bubbles. Ladybug immediately flings her yo-yo at the wand, lassoing it and pulling it back toward her.

She grabs the wand and snaps it in two over her knee. The offending akuma flies out. "Get out of here, you nasty bug!" she says. "No more evildoing for you, little akuma."

Ladybug opens her yo-yo and throws it at the escaping akuma. "Time to de-evilize!" she cries as the yo-yo closes around the bug and snaps shut, trapping the akuma inside. "Gotcha!"

Ladybug opens the yo-yo and the akuma, now transformed back into a beautiful white butterfly, flutters away.

"Bye-bye, little butterfly!"

Ladybug throws the wrench high into the air and shouts, "*Miraculous Ladybug!*"

The wrench transforms into a huge swarm of magical ladybugs. The ladybugs fly across the city's skies, transporting the green bubbles safely to the ground, where they pop and free their prisoners.

Marinette's parents hug each other happily on the sidewalk outside their bakery. Up on the landing, the Bubbler transforms back into a very confused Nino. He sits up and rubs his head, blinking in astonishment.

"Huh?" he mumbles. "Who? *Duuuude…*"

Nearby, Ladybug and Cat Noir fist-bump each other, happy with their work.

"Pound it!"

Back in his lair, Hawk Moth is furious. He once again has had his plans foiled by Ladybug and Cat Noir!

"You can't run forever, Ladybug," he seethes. "And when I catch you, I will crush you! I will destroy you *both*!"

• • •

It's the end of a very long day, and back at Adrien's now-quiet mansion, Nathalie is doing some last-minute work on the computer. Her intercom flashes and Gabriel's face appears.

"Nathalie?" he says. "Did my son like his gift?"

Nathalie's eyes widen as she realizes that she forgot to give Adrien the present the girl dropped off earlier in the day.

"Uhh—actually—um—" she stammers. "I was going to check right away, sir!"

"Good," Gabriel says sharply before hanging up.

Nathalie picks up Marinette's present, still on her desk, and notices the note stuck to it. It reads "Love, Marinette." Beside it, Marinette has drawn a picture of a birthday cake. Nathalie frowns, rips off the note, and throws it into the trash can beside her desk.

Adrien is eating dinner alone in the dining room when Nathalie hurries in with the present in her hands. She composes herself as she approaches him.

"A birthday present," she says in her most professional voice as she holds out the present. "From your father."

Adrien's mouth hangs open. *Father bought me a present?* he thinks. *I can't believe it.*

"Oh…thank you!" Adrien says, taking the gift from her and staring at it in shock. "I mean, please say thank you to my father for me!"

Nathalie feels slightly guilty but simply nods back over her shoulder as Adrien gazes with delight at the gift in his hands.

• • •

The next morning, Chloé yells at a very nervous and trembling Sabrina on the school steps as Alya and Marinette watch in horror.

"What do you mean 'not for a week'?!" Chloé demands.

"There were no adults around yesterday to deliver it," Sabrina squeaks. She holds up her phone as if it will protect her from Chloé's wrath.

"So *what*?!" Chloé shrieks angrily at her. "Ridiculous! Utterly *ridiculous*!"

Chloé stomps away and into the school, with Sabrina scurrying behind her.

"Haha!" Alya laughs. "Serves Chloé right."

"Hey, girls!"

Alya and Marinette turn to see Adrien waving at them as he gets out of his limousine. Marinette feels as if she might faint when she notices her present wrapped around his neck.

"Hey, that's my scarf!" she whispers excitedly to Alya as she waves back at Adrien. "He's wearing my scarf!"

Adrien approaches Nino and fist-bumps his now back-to-normal best friend.

"Hey, dude," Adrien says.

"Yo!" Alya calls out. "Nice scarf, Adrien! Off the chain!"

"Yeah," Adrien says proudly. "Can you believe my dad got this for me?"

Marinette, still waving, instantly freezes. A watermelon-size lump begins to form in her throat.

"It's so awesome," Adrien continues, beaming. "He's given me the same lame pen for three years in a row!"

"Wow!" Nino says, looking impressed. "I guess anyone *can* change. Adults can be cool when you least expect it."

"Speaking of adults," Adrien says, bowing his head and looking embarrassed. "I know my father said you were a bad influence, but—"

"Hey, we're good, Adrien," Nino interrupts, placing a hand on his friend's shoulder. "Don't sweat it! We're buds! Always and forever!"

Nino slings his arm around Adrien's shoulder, and the two friends walk up the stairs.

Alya turns to Marinette. "You've gotta tell him you're the one who knitted the scarf!"

"But he seems so happy about his dad,"

Marinette says, a smile on her face as she watches Adrien walk into school. "I don't want to spoil it for him."

Alya considers her friend for a moment, then reaches over and hugs her warmly.

"Oh, Marinette," she says. "You're amazing, girl. You know that, right?"

Marinette laughs and hugs her back.

The school bell rings and they pull apart. Alya takes Marinette's face in her hands and looks in her eyes. "And someday, Adrien will figure it out, too," she says. "Promise."

The two best friends walk up the stairs together, ready for whatever new adventures the day has in store for them.

ZAG HEROEZ
Miraculous

Time to de-evilize!

For information on Miraculous Fashion Dolls & more toys, please visit:

MIRACULOUSLADYBUG.COM | PLAYMATESTOYS.COM

Playmates ZAG

© 2021 ZAGTOON – METHOD – ALL RIGHTS RESERVED. ©2021 Playmates.